Máquinas maravillosas/Mighty Machines

Camiones con tráiler/Semitrucks

por/by Matt Doeden

Traducción/Translation: Dr. Martín Luis Guzmán Ferrer
Editor Consultor/Consulting Editor: Dra. Gail Saunders-Smith

Consultor/Consultant: Sandy Hurlbut, President
Transportation Center for Excellence
Eagan, Minnesota

Capstone
press®

Mankato, Minnesota

Pebble Plus is published by Capstone Press,
151 Good Counsel Drive, P.O. Box 669, Mankato, Minnesota 56002.
www.capstonepress.com

1 2 3 4 5 6 12 11 10 09 08 07

Library of Congress Cataloging-in-Publication Data
Doeden, Matt.
    [Semitrucks. Spanish & English]
    Camiones con tráiler/por Matt Doeden = Semitrucks/by Matt Doeden.
    p. cm.—(Pebble plus—máquinas maravillosas = Pebble plus—mighty machines)
    Includes index.
    Summary: "Simple text and photographs present semitrucks, their parts, and how drivers use
them—in both English and Spanish"—Provided by publisher.
    ISBN-13: 978-0-7368-7644-5 (hardcover : alk. paper)
    ISBN-10: 0-7368-7644-8 (hardcover : alk. paper)
    1. Tractor trailer combinations—Juvenile literature. I. Title.
TL230.15.D64518 2007
629.224—dc22   2006027791

Editorial Credits
Amber Bannerman, editor; Katy Kudela, bilingual editor; Eida del Risco, Spanish copy editor; Molly Nei,
    set designer; Patrick D. Dentinger, book designer; Jo Miller, photo researcher; Scott Thoms, photo editor

Photo Credits
Capstone Press/TJ Thoraldson Digital Photography, cover (truck), 4–5, 6–7, 10–11, 12–13
Corbis/zefa/Roland Gerth, 20–21
The Image Finders/Mark E. Gibson, 16–17
Photodisc, cover (fruit)
Shutterstock/David Gaylor, 1
UNICORN Stock Photos/Jeff Greenberg, 9; Martin R. Jones, 18–19; Ted Rose, 14–15

**Capstone Press would like to thank Rob Alvarado (page 10) and the Westman Freightliner company in
    Mankato, Minnesota, for their assistance with photo shoots for this book.**

Note to Parents and Teachers

The Máquinas maravillosas/Mighty Machines set supports national standards related to science, technology, and society. This book describes and illustrates semitrucks in both English and Spanish. The images support early readers in understanding the text. The repetition of words and phrases helps early readers learn new words. This book also introduces early readers to subject-specific vocabulary words, which are defined in the Glossary section. Early readers may need assistance to read some words and to use the Table of Contents, Glossary, Internet Sites, and Index sections of the book.

Table of Contents

Tabla de contenidos

What Are Semitrucks?

Semitrucks are

big, strong trucks.

They pull trailers

and deliver goods to stores.

¿Qué son los camiones con tráiler?

Los camiones con tráiler son unos

camiones grandes y pesados.

Jalan remolques y entregan

mercancías a las tiendas.

Semitruck Parts

The front part

of a semitruck

is called the tractor.

The engine is in the tractor.

Las partes de un camión con tráiler

La parte delantera de

un camión con tráiler se

llama tractor. El motor

está en el tractor.

engine/motor

The trailer hooks onto

the back of the tractor.

The trailer holds boxes

of food, clothing,

and other goods.

El remolque se engancha a

la parte trasera del tractor.

El remolque lleva cajas de

comida, ropa y otras mercancías.

Most semitrucks
have 18 wheels.
Some have 10 wheels.

La mayoría de los camiones
con tráiler tienen 18 ruedas.
Algunos camiones con tráiler
tienen 10 ruedas.

The driver sits in the cab.
All the truck's controls
are inside the cab.

El chofer se sienta en la cabina.
Todos los mandos del tráiler están
dentro de la cabina.

What Semitrucks Do

Semitrucks pull heavy loads.

They move cars

from place to place.

Para qué sirven los camiones con tráiler

Los camiones con tráiler

transportan cargas muy pesadas.

También trasportan autos de

un lugar a otro.

Some semitrucks
haul tankers.
Tankers are filled with
gasoline or other liquids.

Algunos camiones con
tráiler remolcan cisternas.
Las cisternas están llenas de
gasolina o de otros líquidos.

Some semitrucks
carry buildings.
They may even
haul other trucks.

Algunos camiones con
tráiler transportan casas.
Y hasta pueden remolcar
otros camiones.

Mighty Semitrucks

A semitruck pulls
a heavy load.
Semitrucks are
mighty machines.

Maravillosos camiones con tráiler

Un camión con tráiler
jala una pesada carga.
Los camiones con tráiler son
unas máquinas maravillosas.

Glossary

cab—an enclosed area of a truck or other vehicle where the driver sits

engine—a machine that makes the power needed to move something

goods—the items people buy, sell, and use; semitrucks deliver goods to stores.

haul—to pull or carry a load

tanker—a trailer that holds liquids, such as gasoline or milk

trailer—the part of a semitruck where goods are loaded and carried

Glosario

la cabina—parte cubierta de un camión u
otro vehículo

la cisterna—remolque que trasporta líquidos,
como gasolina o leche

las mercancías—artículos que la gente compra,
vende y usa; los camiones con tráiler entregan
mercancías a las tiendas.

el motor—máquina que produce la energía para
mover algo

remolcar—transportar o tirar de una carga

el remolque—parte del camión con tráiler donde
se cargan las mercancías y se transportan

Internet Sites

FactHound offers a safe, fun way to find Internet sites related to this book. All of the sites on FactHound have been researched by our staff.

Here's how:

1. Visit *www.facthound.com*

2. Choose your grade level.

3. Type in this book ID **0736876448** for age-appropriate sites. You may also browse subjects by clicking on letters, or by clicking on pictures and words.

4. Click on the **Fetch It** button.

FactHound will fetch the best sites for you!

Index

Sitios de Internet

FactHound proporciona una manera divertida y segura de encontrar sitios de Internet relacionados con este libro. Nuestro personal ha investigado todos los sitios de FactHound. Es posible que los sitios no estén en español.

Se hace así:

1. Visita *www.facthound.com*

2. Elige tu grado escolar.

3. Introduce este código especial **0736876448** para ver sitios apropiados según tu edad, o usa una palabra relacionada con este libro para hacer una búsqueda general.

4. Haz clic en el botón **Fetch It**.

¡FactHound buscará los mejores sitios para ti!

Índice